GET READY...GET SET...READ!

SNOW IN JULY

by
Foster & Erickson

Illustrations by
Kerri Gifford

FOREST HOUSE ™
School & Library Edition

"It's too hot for ball,"
said Stonewall—
"too hot in my stall."

"Yes," said Snowball.
"It's too hot in the wall."

"It's hot on the mound
and it's hot underground,"
said Groundhog.

"Our row is so hot,
we cannot grow,"
said Ludlow.

5

"I wish it would snow
this July," said Small Fry.

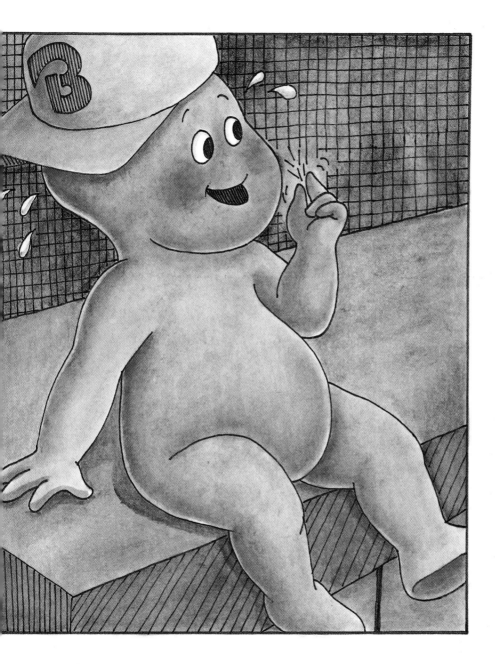

"Maybe we could use
Matthew's brew!"
said Bartholomew.

"The magic brew can make
walking things fly."

"Well then, why not
snow in July?"

"Let's try!"
said Small Fry.

So Bartholomew threw
some brew into the sky.

A butterfly went flying by—
but no snow.

A dragonfly went flying by—
the wind began to blow.

A firefly went flying by—
it felt like ten below.

Then it happened—
there was snow!

The snow made no sound
as it hit the ground.

Soon the snow was all around.

"I can't catch it,"
said Groundhog.
"It flies right by."

"Catch this!"
said Small Fry.
And he let a snowball fly.

19

"Look out below, Ludlow!"
said Bartholomew.

Then Ludlow wound up and
threw one at Bartholomew.

"That's great," said Stonewall.
"Let's play ball." Bam!

"Come here and see
what I've found,"
said Hound.

"The water is hard,
as hard as the ground."

"Oh my," said Snowball.
"I'm flying without even trying."

Then Snowball took a fall.
She rolled round and round.

"So that's why you're called
Snowball," said Hound.

Then the sky began to glow,
and the snow began to go.

"Thank you Bartholomew,
we don't know how or why,
but you did it."

"You made snow in July!"

DEAR PARENTS AND EDUCATORS:

Welcome to **Get Ready...Get Set...Read!**

We've created these books to introduce children to the magic of reading.

Each story in the series is built around one or two word families. For example, *A Mop for Pop* uses the OP word family. Letters and letter blends are added to OP to form words such as TOP, LOP, and STOP.

This **Bring-It-All-Together** book serves as a reading review. When your children have finished *Tall and Small, Bounder's Sound, How to Catch a Butterfly, Ludlow Grows Up,* and *Matthew's Brew*, it is time to have them read this book. *Snow in July* uses some of the characters and most of the words introduced in the fifth set of five **Get Ready . . . Get Set . . . Read!** stories. (Each set in the series will be followed by two review books.)

Bring-It-All-Together books provide:
- much needed vocabulary repetition for developing fluency.
- longer stories for increasing reading attention spans.
- new stories with familiar characters for motivating young readers.

We have created these **Bring-It-All-Together** books to help develop confidence and competence in your young reader. We wish you much success in your reading adventures.

Kelli C. Foster, Ph.D.   Gina Clegg Erickson, MA
Educational Psychologist   Reading Specialist

All inquiries should be addressed to:
Barron's Educational Series, Inc.
250 Wireless Boulevard
Hauppauge, NY 11788

International Standard Book Number 0-8120-9336-4
Library of Congress Catalog Card Number: 95-51731

PRINTED IN HONG KONG
6789   9927   987654321

Titles in the

Series:

SET 1

Find Nat
The Sled Surprise
Sometimes I Wish
A Mop for Pop
The Bug Club
BRING-IT-ALL-TOGETHER BOOKS
What a Day for Flying!
Bat's Surprise

SET 2

The Tan Can
The Best Pets Yet
Pip and Kip
Frog Knows Best
Bub and Chub
BRING-IT-ALL-TOGETHER BOOKS
Where Is the Treasure?
What a Trip!

SET 3

Jake and the Snake
Jeepers Creepers
Two Fine Swine
What Rose Doesn't Know
Pink and Blue
BRING-IT-ALL-TOGETHER BOOKS
The Pancake Day
Hide and Seek

SET 4

Whiptail of Blackshale Trail
Colleen and the Bean
Dwight and the Trilobite
The Old Man at the Moat
By the Light of the Moon
BRING-IT-ALL-TOGETHER BOOKS
Night Light
The Crossing

SET 5

Tall and Small
Bounder's Sound
How to Catch a Butterfly
Ludlow Grows Up
Matthew's Brew
BRING-IT-ALL-TOGETHER BOOKS
Snow in July
Let's Play Ball*

* Forthcoming title